CW00859805

Dedicated to...
The 'real' Squiggles
and all the boys and girls
just like him

Acknowledgements

A massive thank you to Dr Gavin Reid for diagnosing my son's Dyslexia and highlighting his other educational strengths and weaknesses.

A huge thank you to Gloria Morgan of Dayglo Books for all your valuable advice and encouragement for this labour of love.

Many thanks to Andy Cook, CEO of Helen Arkell Dyslexia Charity, for your words of support and encouragement.

* * *

First published
in 2021 by
DESERT♥HEARTS
www.deserthearts.com

© Susan Stewart 2021
Illustrations © Nick Awde 2021

Typeset & designed by Desert♥Hearts
Typeset in Abelardo Gonzalez's Open Dyslexic font

Printed and bound in Great Britain by Printforce

British Library Cataloguing in Publication Data
A catalogue record for this book is available from
the British Library

ISBN 9781908755445

Any similarity to living people is coincidental in this book.

Caution
This book is sold subject to the condition that it shall not, by way of
trade or otherwise, be lent, resold, hired out, or otherwise circulated
without the publisher's prior consent in any form of binding or cover
other than that in which it is published and without a similar
condition being imposed on the subsequent purchaser.

Dog-Lexius

A Tale of Two Friends

Susan Stewart

Illustrations by Nick Awde

DESERT ♥ HEARTS

1

Sam is nine and hates reading.

People tell him it's because he's a boy and boys don't enjoy reading, but Sam knows that's not true. He knows at least two girls who would rather be climbing trees than reading.

Sam is aware that he can't read as well as his friends, and he doesn't know why.

Sam had asked his Teacher if she knew why. His Teacher said he was fine. But Sam's Mum knows he is struggling at school. She wants to help.

Sam would love to have a dog. Harvey, his old dog, died when he was six. His Mum said if he tries harder with reading, they can re-home one from the shelter. But trying harder only leaves Sam feeling more confused.

He loves his computer and enjoys creating space games, and he has an endless imagination that brings wonderful characters to life.

Sam would prefer to use a computer for his school work, but his Head Teacher wants him to improve his poor handwriting skills first... Boring!

And then one evening after another challenging day at school, Sam finished his dinner and went upstairs to his bedroom.

It was a hot July day and the heat was making everything an effort. He pushed the bedroom window open a little further, then sat down in front of his computer.

Sam decided to create his very own space puppy!

2

The evening had flown by and Sam had fallen fast asleep dreaming of the new doggie friend he had created on his computer.

On her way to bed, Mum stopped by Sam's bedroom to turn off his bedside light and kiss him good night.

He had fallen into a deep slumber before he could think of a brilliant name for the space pup. He didn't want something too soft, and it had to have **meaning**. Sam had been named after his Dad, who sadly died before he was born.

As the hands on the bedroom clock came together at midnight, he woke suddenly.

Had he heard a loud sneeze close by?

Sure that he was dreaming, he lay back down. But just as he did, from the end of his bed yapped a kind voice in the darkness.

"Excuse me, it's the dust." There was another sneeze, and then... "Do you want to go on an adventure, Sam?"

Sitting up, he rubbed his tired eyes to make sure he was actually awake.

He could barely utter a word. There at the end of his bed, sitting on his new blue and white striped duvet, was a very excited, middle-aged Jack Russell Terrier!

"I'm dreaming," Sam said.

"You're not dreaming!" said the cheeky-looking hound. "I'm Dog-Lexius."

"Dog-Lexius?"

"Yes, you created me on your computer."

Sam was properly awake now, his eyes wide open with delight.

Around the dog's neck was a bright blue collar. The name 'Dog-Lexius' was engraved on the bone-shaped tag that dangled from a metal ring.

Sam remembered designing the tag on his computer, but he also remembered that he hadn't decided on a name. He also knew he had not created the tiny red rucksack attached to the little dog's back. It appeared to flicker as if it were filled with magic.

Dog-Lexius stretched out his neck and had a good scratch under his fluffy white chin.

"No need to be scared, Sam. I know all about you, lad. It's no coincidence I came to life from your thoughts. Just press my name tag and off we go. Hurry though, we don't have long!"

Sam noticed the little dog glance

down at his watch. Its brightly coloured numbers looked kind of cool.

"Long for what?" Sam asked. "What's up?"

"Do you know what Dyslexia is?"

"Ummm... Dyslexia?" Sam was confused.

"Dyslexia is something which makes letters and numbers play games with our brain. It affects how many people understand and process things. Dyslexia makes reading and writing difficult.

"You're Dyslexic, Sam, and I want to help you. I want you to understand why you are struggling at school."

The bone-shaped tag on Dog-Lexius's collar started flashing and swirling like a Catherine wheel on Fireworks Night.

Sam's heart was now pounding so loudly he thought it would wake up his Mum in the next bedroom.

"Ready? Let's have some fun!" said

the little dog with a toothy grin that
ran from ear to ear.

Without another thought, Sam
leaned forward and pressed the tag
on his new friend's collar as quickly
as his trembling fingers would allow.

3

Once the array of hypnotising colours stopped swirling around him, Sam found himself sitting in a space ship.

He had been magically transported out of his bedroom window and far into the night sky.

"Where are we going Dog-Lexius?"

Dog-Lexius beamed. "You'll see! And please, just call me Lexius, Sam."

Whizzing through the solar system with eyes so wide they almost popped, Sam could barely hold on to his thoughts – or his hair!

They challenged shooting stars at high speed. They swooped over mysterious planets. Loop-the-looping the moon was an awesome experience. All things that he would never forget. And that nobody would ever believe!

Relaxing a little, Sam took notice of their spacecraft. Chuckling to himself, he saw that it had all the makings of a supercharged Flying Water Bowl. **A water bowl!** But it was filled to the brim with gadgets and technology that a child could only dream of.

Sam suddenly thought of Matty, his best friend. When the fair came to town every Easter and summer, they would spend most of their pocket money on the waltzer or the tea cup rides.

They did everything fun together – and this was definitely **fun!**

He could see every planet dazzling brightly, and he couldn't help wondering if this was especially for him.

On they flew, soaring past Jupiter, spinning across Mars, swooping over Pluto. And since he was only nine, Sam couldn't stop the wide grin that instantly hijacked his face when they slowed up alongside the planet Uranus.

Something extremely bright began glowing in the distance. As they drew closer, Sam could see three rings – two purple and one green.

Lexius was frantically tapping coordinates into his Paw-Pad. But the Flying Water Bowl appeared to be in control of itself now.

Sam started to wonder if something had gone wrong.

"Keep calm lad, everything is OK!" yapped Lexius. "The rings have such a powerful force that pulls us in. They tend to over-ride my coordinates and once we have impact we will probably spin a little off-track. The purple rings are strong Sam. Having two makes doubly sure we don't miss the planet."

"And the green ring, Lexius – what does that do? It's **really bright!**"

"It's meant to be. It's like a giant torch. The green ring lights up the sky, assisting our arrival."

The Flying Water Bowl hurtled like a magnet towards the rings and the planet they were circling!

Lexius dropped his Paw-Pad and leaped forwards. Pressing his wet nose and front two paws against the protective glass shell of the Flying Water Bowl, he watched intently as they began their rapid descent.

"Where are we?" asked Sam, following the dog's gaze down towards the fast approaching rings and the purple-looking planet below.

But before Lexius could answer, a slight whistle was heard seconds before the Flying Water Bowl filled with the smell of a cheese sandwich that had been forgotten about for at least a month!

Lexius popped a glance at his tail end, but said nothing.

"No time for questions lad, just hold on! It's often a slippery landing. The power force here is intense. We have to hit the planet right on that dark green spot, or risk being spun out into the galaxy and we'll probably be lost forever! The moment we have impact, the light from the green ring will instantly shut down."

Sam squeezed his eyes shut at the thought. His hands stopped covering his nose and instead gripped firmly on the metal safety bar that had automatically drawn around them when they entered the Flying Water Bowl.

The audio navigation system had now become irritatingly stuck, repeatedly announcing: "You have now reached your destination! You have now reached your destination! You have now reached your destination...!"

Braced for a crash-landing, Sam and his new companion were ready for impact, as the planet's surface filled their view until it was close enough to touch.

The Flying Water Bowl hit the dark

green spot and the light from the green ring went out, just as Lexius had said it would. They slid a long way before clipping a large rock. The craft instantly rolled onto its side, flipping out both boy and dog like pancakes onto a blanket of the most enchanting silvery blue dust.

Sparkling particles glittered the atmosphere, giving them light whilst also announcing their clumsy entry to the planet.

Gathering himself up, Sam brushed the twinkling dust from his pyjamas.

Spinning 360 degrees in panic, he called out for his dog companion.

In the distance, illuminated by the extremely sparkly fragments, Lexius emerged like a dancing shadow from a heap of glimmering dust which had buried him completely upon landing.

He trotted over to Sam with a cheeky wink and a thumbs up.

The scruffy hound then did a

doggy-like shimmy, ridding his coat of all the dusty sparkles he had collected along the way. He completed a good scratch behind both ears before declaring he was good to go.

"I can't imagine how I passed my landing test!" he said with a grin. "You OK?"

"Err... yes, I feel brilliant," said Sam a bit confused. Was there really such a thing as a landing test for a Flying Water Bowl, he found himself wondering.

"Welcome to Letter Land, Sam!" bellowed Lexius, swinging his arms wide in front of his chest. "This is the land where Letters don't always behave. We are going on a long journey tonight. In fact you have an appointment with Geraldine the Letter Goblin, so we'd best get a move on.

"The Letter Goblin lives at the top

of Letter Mountain, and Syia, the brightest, most special star of all reigns over the mountain."

"I can't see a mountain or a star, Lexius," said Sam, looking into the dusky distance. All he could see was trees, lots of TREES!

"Ahh, no lad, you can't see either of them from here. Letter Mountain is quite some way away and Syia shines directly onto the Mountain. But you will see them, and believe me, the journey will definitely be worth it.

"The Syia star radiates love. And with love comes unconditional acceptance. Syia's strength is the greatest power there is. The Goblins use her power to understand and help children like you.

"The Letter Goblin understands that not all children can read and write properly. She believes that all children deserve the chance to be understood."

4

The deep forest lay ahead of them. A strange sense of sadness seemed to creep out towards them from its edges.

Sam, however, felt excitement tingling in his legs.

Standing before the thick darkness of the trees, Sam could not quite take in the sight of what was now happening.

His mouth gaped wide open as in the half-light he watched Lexius busy pulling two pairs of bright green snow boots, two small yet very yellow Boogie-type boards and two pairs of goggles from his miniature rucksack. It was like watching a magician pull rabbits out of a hat.

"You up for some tree-surfing, Sam? These boards are designed to travel at great speed across those treetops. Don't worry, the boots have magnetic strips that keep you safely attached to your board. They activate the moment you stand on the board. They'll keep your feet toasty too.

"Now, these galaxy goggles are paramount. If a star bursts up there we may be caught in its intense solar blast which will cause us to surf off track. Should you end up in a black hole, blink twice quickly and the goggle sensors will activate black hole night vision and navigation."

Sam's mouth was still hanging open. Lexius extended a paw and gently closed it shut.

Now a bit more focused, Sam saw one of the two purple rings in the sky above them starting to fade.

"Why is the ring disappearing?"

"The rings only glow together for thirty minutes at midnight, ready for your arrival. Both will be gone soon. They become alight again for another thirty minutes at 5 a.m., just in time to power you back home.

"The green light will beam out again then too. Letter Land knows how the darkness can be a very scary thing for you little ones. It's extremely important that you complete your mission and return here back to the Flying Water Bowl on time. If you are late and the rings have started to fade, they will not have enough strength to power you home. Your Mum will raise the alarm that you are missing, and that will simply never do!"

So they quickly pulled on their boots and put the goggles over their eyes.

"Activate your night vision, Sam,"

Lexius instructed. "It's still quite dark and I don't want you surfing off in the wrong direction and getting lost!"

Sam blinked twice. Instantly everything around him became clear and in focus, floodlit by a luminous yellow.

Tucking a tree-surfing board firmly under an arm, the pair headed off in the direction of the trees.

At the edge of the forest they placed their boards on the shimmering dust. Lexius's wet doggie nose started to twitch. His thin black lips pulled up tight towards his gums displaying most of his teeth.

"Huh-huh-huh-**chooo**!!"

As Lexius sneezed, Sam felt a combination of snot and saliva splatter against the back of his hand.

"It's the dust lad, it gets right up my nose. Stand on your board, Sam, and do like I do."

"Ee-errrr..." Wiping his hand

discreetly on his pyjama bottoms, Sam stood on his board and put one foot in front of the other.

"Crouch down and pull out the little silver lever on the right side of the board."

Again Sam did as Lexius instructed.

"The faster you move the lever out determines how fast you go. Pull it up to go up, push down to go down. OK, lad, got it?"

"Yes, got it," said Sam, a little unsure.

Pulling the lever up slowly, Sam levitated off the glimmering dust.

"Hey Lexius, look at me. I'm up! I'm in the air!" cried Sam.

Lexius turned to speak just as Sam pulled the lever outwards. Shooting off like a rocket, the eager boy went headfirst into a round prickly bush that sat minding its own business on the edge of the forest.

"Slow down, Sam! Get used to it.

Get your balance!" said Lexius, shaking his head.

Sam straightened up his goggles, plucked a couple of prickles out of his shoulder and one from his cheek, before walking back to Lexius.

They stood on their boards together. Sam used more caution, placing his feet further apart for balance. He exercised more control over his hand that was operating the lever and finally, after a few wobbles here and there, he gradually rose up to join Lexius in the night sky.

Gliding over the treetops, Sam felt a bit like Santa Claus on Christmas Eve. Did Santa still get excited, flying around the world in his merry sleigh?

Sam felt his cheeks turning rosy. Yes, he was nervous but he loved the exhilarating feeling rushing through his body as they sped along.

He felt the soft pitter-pattering of glitter-dust against his face as a moon rock exploded somewhere in the distance below them.

Tree-surfing was awesome and Sam embraced every second. But his youthful legs were already starting to tire from the continuous bent stance they had adopted in order to ride the boards over the uneven treetops.

"Sam, look down!" Lexius shouted, whooping as he pointed. "See the names engraved in the branches? They're street names. Slow down and look for 'Per Contra Gardens'."

"Per Con— what? Lexius" Sam asked.

"Gardens. 'Per Contra' Gardens! It means 'On the Contrary' in Latin – it's kind of like your struggles at school, Sam. You need to learn in a more unique way to most other children in your class, but that's cool—"

And in that split second, Sam lost all concentration. He wobbled this way and that way. He swayed left to right and left again, before finally toppling off his board.

The silver birch tree offered Sam a safe landing, extending one of its massive branches in hospitality, breaking his fall.

Sam landed with a heavy thump, right, as luck would have it, on to Per Contra Gardens.

He sat a little dazed, amongst a crisscross of other street names.

As soon as Lexius landed, he began stuffing the boards back inside his magical rucksack. The goggles stayed comfortably on their foreheads.

Suddenly the tree's silver bark began cracking, it rippled one way and then rumbled the other until the tree broke open, revealing a familiar setting.

The street where Sam lived stretched out before him. He saw the alleyway leading to his local swing park and playing field. Pretty, tidy borders would show it was cared for by the 'Friends' of his neighbourhood.

Bollards stood at the road's entrance, denying cars access, and

although he couldn't see it, Sam
knew his school sat just the other
side of the playing field.

5

How could something so small have so much authority, wondered Sam, as the little silver whistle pierced the air! Skipping ropes were dropped back into plastic storage boxes. Footballs were kicked towards the play shed.

Mrs Humphrys, Mrs Holmes and Mr Keen stood patiently whilst ninety-six children began lining up neatly, ready to go back to class. Two young boys in Mrs Humphrys' class gravitated towards each other, causing the end of her line of thirty-two to look messy.

"Thomas and Harry!" Mrs Humphrys screeched. "Please behave!"

The click-clack of her shoes on the tarmac was a worrying sound as she walked up to the boys.

Mrs Humphrys plucked Thomas like a stray eyebrow from the line. Spinning on her heels with the ends of her hair taking flight, she marched the children back inside, with Thomas now walking neatly behind her at the very front.

Sam and Lexius peered in through the large classroom windows, as the children began to settle at their desks.

Mrs Humphrys began walking around the classroom handing everyone a copy of the same book. She explained that everyone was to take their turn in reading a couple of sentences out loud.

Clara was instructed to start – and 'Clever' Clara read with ease. Meanwhile an issue involving Thomas and Harry started to escalate in the back row.

Lexius gave Sam a look. "See anything familiar, lad?"

"Thomas is like me, isn't he?" Sam observed.

As they watched, Thomas, desperate to evade reading aloud, continually took Harry's pencil.

Harry, now having Mrs Humphrys' full attention, began whining that the black and yellow HB pencil was rightfully his, and that he had had enough of Thomas's behaviour.

Thomas was once again moved to the front row, and Mrs Humphrys announced it was so she could keep a good eye on him.

Unfortunately for Thomas, his urge to ask Mrs Humphrys "which of her eyes was the good one" cost him the first ten minutes of his next playtime.

Bemused and feeling more lost than ever, Thomas sat slumped analysing his knees, whilst considering if his school days would have been more comfortable had he been in Mr Keen's class.

"My Teacher says I have 'no filter'," said Sam. "But I say what I see or feel. Why is that wrong?"

"It's not wrong, Sam. It's just that some folks take it as rude. You are an observant lad – and that's OK!"

Sam battled the emotional lump that formed in his throat. "It's reading aloud that makes me nervous. I can't control myself like the others. No one understands how difficult it is for me. And then my Teacher says, 'Why don't you try to be more like Matty at school?'" Sam made his voice high and airy as he pretended to be like his Teacher.

"Matty's my best friend, he's in the top set for reading. Matty's brain understands phonics. He can pronounce lots of tricky words, without needing to stop and sound them out. And my Teacher thinks reading is easy too! She thinks I'm just naughty. And now my Mum is worried about me."

A tear broke free from the watery glaze that blurred Sam's vision. He didn't try to stop it from gliding down his cheek. The innocent droplet froze momentarily, quivering on his chin, then fell, breaking on the window sill.

Lexius extended a fluffy paw and Sam felt five spiky claws squeeze gently into his shoulder.

"Sam...," Lexius began. "You are struggling with the everyday problems that Dyslexia causes, and sadly your Teacher isn't noticing the signs."

"I try, Lexius, I really do. So many words just don't make sense to me. They can be so hard to pronounce. And my handwriting isn't great either.

Even I can't always read what I've written! My Teacher says I'm not giving her my best, but my hand hurts from trying. Reading and writing make me feel sad. I just want to be like my friends..."

"You shouldn't wish to be the same as everyone else," said Lexius gently. "We're all unique, and that's how it should be. At school there will always be a child who challenges what others think is right or normal. Unfortunately it's these children that can fall behind with their education. Matty learns in one way and you in another, but you are all equal. You must believe that, Sam."

The young boy's face started to scrunch up. He took a couple of short sharp breaths inwards, and Lexius knew Sam was about to burst into tears.

Eager to spare his new friend this sadness, Lexius tried his best to comfort him with words of wisdom. "Awww come now, lad, lose that look, please don't cry. I know it's difficult now, but there's a great big world waiting for you out there. School is challenging, but it's really only a stepping stone to the rest of your life, so you must enjoy it and learn what you can. You're a bright boy, Sam. You're great with computers, and that's an amazing skill.

"So come on, let's be on our way. Let's put a smile back on that jolly face of yours!"

6

"**Up, up and away!**" shouted Sam.

The pair laughed, exhilarated as the boards carried them away. On they surfed, to the next instalment of the craziest night Sam would probably ever know!

Sam stole a glance back over his shoulder. He saw the tree's mighty branches weaving tightly back together again, keeping their world safe from intruders. Whoever they may be...

"Where are we going now?" Sam called to Lexius who was speeding ahead of him.

"We're going to the deepest part

of the forest!" Lexius shouted back, tilting his head up towards the stars. "We're going to where the Woodpecker dwells. She will transport us to the Frozen Land. She will set us on the path to the Letter Goblin."

Sam considered the possibility that he was still asleep and hallucinating. Was Mum right? She had caught him sneaking his favourite chocolate bar up to bed and she had explained to him how it wasn't a good idea to eat sugar before going to sleep.

Was this the effects of a sugar rush? Next time he would think twice before ignoring his Mum!

Sam pinched himself hard on his arm to see if he was awake or dreaming. He was awake, because it hurt!

They hadn't been surfing for long before the tightly packed leaves below them began to unravel once more. This time they transformed into a path of fast moving shiny yellow arrows. They were leading him towards his next destination.

"**Use your lever Sam. Start slowing down!**" Lexius bellowed.

Sam gulped loudly as he came to a halt beside Lexius. He watched the never-ending flow of arrows falling rapidly away below them.

"What do we do here. Where are the arrows leading to?" Sam asked. He was trying to keep his breath calm and regain control of his nerves. "Are the arrows showing us the way to somewhere?" he quizzed, continuing to hover in the night sky.

"They are flowing down to the Alphabet River, Sam. It's your route to the Woodpecker. It's the only way I'm afraid, lad. Try not to worry, you can do it. Don't think, just go with the flow! The fall isn't as steep as it looks. Just a couple of speedy seconds and we will be beside the river. Do you want to go first or second?"

"Umm, first I think. No, wait, second! I'll follow you."

"Cool. I'll meet you by the Alphabet River in a second or three. But hurry, Sam, the time is ticking. We need to catch a Letter Boat. We must be at the Enchanted Cove before the Woodpecker takes flight.

"The Woodpecker is the Letter Goblin's communication network. Once she senses you nearby, she'll peck out a signal onto the bark of the ancient Wanna-Wanna Tree. The vibrations travel across the land. They let the Letter Goblin know you have arrived.

"The Woodpecker will surround us in a blanket of warm light that will protect us from the harsh chill that is holding Letter Land captive."

"But why is Letter Land being held captive?" Sam asked.

Lexius looked at his watch. "All will become apparent soon, lad. **Now let's goooo!**"

Sam's stomach somersaulted as he followed the crazy dog and the arrows over the edge!

7

The arrows flowed gracefully into the river. Sam on the other hand, plunged awkwardly off his board, demonstrating a very messy roly-poly as he hit the riverbank.

Lexius landed beside him, just as gracefully as the yellow arrows hit the water. But then, he had had a lot of practice over the years.

The pair now sat together at the water's edge.

Sitting, starring at the most splendid river he had ever seen, Sam began to take in what was happening.

Studying the water, he saw some of the Letters that made his reading and writing difficult.

First, floating angelically came the troublesome B that pretends to be a D. It floated at ease. No apology for the stress it causes.

Then, without a care in the world, came the OO's. Bobbing along like ducks they were unaware of the stress they caused on a daily basis.

And as they drifted by, IS and TH seemed as if they waved!

Sam had tried explaining to his Teacher how some Letters moved around in a blur on his page. Sadly this had only been acknowledged with a heavy sigh, a sigh so powerful it sent the Teacher's eyebrows levitating into her fringe!

The two new friends sat at the river's edge watching the Letters as they went by.

A soft lapping noise interrupted their thoughts.

Turning together, they were greeted by a yellow S-shaped boat bobbing in the flowing water beside them.

"Get in, get in!" sang the boat. And it started pulling away.

Sam had by now surrendered to whatever was happening. He chose not to question singing boats, alphabet rivers or a cute talking dog with a sneezing habit and a Flying Water Bowl anymore tonight.

He trusted morning would come and when it did, all this might, or might not, make some kind of sense.

8

"**Jump in!**" Lexius howled, his chin stretched high towards the sky as he clambered aboard the boat. "**It's nearly 1.30 in the morning! Sam, we need this boat! We can't wait for another!**"

Sam landed in the shallow curve of the S-Boat where Lexius was already perched on one of its little S-shaped seats. But the impact of Sam's clumsy landing flung Lexius up in to the air and headfirst went the little dog into the river.

Lexius absolutely loathed getting wet. He never saw the need for a shower. A dog, he thought, should carry a subtle 'niff' for the purpose of keeping all cats and certain humans at bay!

Applying some very impressive doggy-paddle, he soon caught up with Sam and the S-boat. Trying to get back onboard, the soggy dog frantically scrabbled and scratched at the side of the boat.

Leaning over the edge, Sam grabbed two handfuls of a very wet and furry waistline and heaved Lexius back inside the boat.

Looking far from impressed, the little terrier dispersed water everywhere as he frantically shook his coat free of the river.

After collapsing at Sam's feet for a few moments, Lexius was soon back up on his paws, full of interest. His fluffy ears stood bolt upright, and his wet nose pointed forwards, as he sprung up and down on the spot like a kangaroo!

"**Tally ho!**" whooped the wet dog, as the current around the S-Boat got suddenly stronger "Come on Sam. Stand up here with me! The river has picked up speed. It's helping you get to the Woodpecker on time. It knows we're running late!"

9

Unmoved by their arrival, the Woodpecker gripped firmly to the side of a very brightly coloured tree. Its vibrant crimson bark and emerald coloured leaves caused the surrounding trees to appear rather humble in its presence.

Immersed in a ball of white light, the bird pecked rhythmically on the trunk's vivid crimson bark.

After finishing her task, the predominantly black and white bird spread her wings and flew towards them in a burst of colour, showing off her beautiful red lower belly. Descending gracefully, she landed on the prow of their little boat.

"She's here to help us, Sam. She's here to help you," Lexius whispered. His head was so close that his wiry whiskers tickled Sam's ear.

With her black, bead-like eyes fixed on Sam, the bird cocked her head and began to sing:

"Go you must! You have
   travelled so far.
Listen with your heart, the
   Goblin's wisdom is true!
Off now to the cold land, you
   have no time to tally,
Your future is thawing, it is
   waiting for you!"

Sam felt his face flush and his toes wobble as a warm breeze gathered beneath his feet. The same warm white glow that lay fog-like around the bird now surrounded the two friends.

Sam felt the gentle warmth on his

body as it lifted them up and away from the boat.

And in that very moment, they were gone!

10

The Blanket of Warmth shielded their bodies from the chill that lay far and wide. Frozen and untouched, a diamond-esque frosting lay out before them, bewitching, glinting in every direction.

"This place is frozen solid, Lexius." Sam couldn't help shivering at the sight.

"It's mimicking your mind, Sam. Once you understand more about yourself and know that Dyslexia is no fault of your own, you will be happier and more fulfilled. Letter Land will once again become a warm and wonderful place to live."

"Where exactly are we then?"

"We have reached the deepest part of Letter Land. Here we'll find the Letter Goblin. The Letter Goblin will help give you the confidence to deal with your struggles. She will help you understand that Dyslexia doesn't define you, you'll see."

A jingling of bells began and six beautiful Husky dogs appeared from nowhere. A sight to captivate any child stood before their eyes: pulling a red and gold sleigh lit with lamps, each dog wore a deep red leather harness.

The Blanket of Warmth gathered them up, lifted them over and settled them into their ride.

Unlike the technology-filled Flying Water Bowl they had left Sam's bedroom in, the sleigh was devoid of gadgets and wizardry. Just one large green button simply stating **'Push Me'** sat between them on the seat.

Sam pushed down firmly on the

button with both his hands. A horn sounded out. The Huskies reared high on their hind legs and did what they were trained to do... **Run!!**

Sam fell back into his seat with a bump.

Around them Jack Frost had certainly worked his chilly magic. It must have taken him hours to create such a spectacular landscape, zapping everything with just his imagination and his ice crook.

A wash of brightly coloured lights gave illumination and glamour to the array of deep green fir trees lining the next stage of their journey.

Sam handed his goggles back to Lexius, who popped them back into the mysterious little rucksack. It was brighter here, they wouldn't be needing them.

Large perfectly formed flakes of snow, the type you only see in fairy tales, began to fall.

"Wow, it's like Christmas time here, Lexius! I love snow! Every time it snows, Matty and I build a great big snowman, first at my house and then at his. We have snowball fights and stuff snow down each other's jackets."

Lexius's heart warmed as Sam's eyes glowed at the memories of playing with his best friend.

The sleigh came to a halt. The Huskies sat back on their hindquarters, as if they knew their part of this night-time mission was complete.

"Why are we stopping? There's nothing here, just ice and trees."

"Patience, lad, Geraldine knows you are here." As Lexius finished speaking, a Goblin village began to unfold right in front of their eyes amidst the trees.

The Blanket of Warmth lifted them out, placing them gently on the ground.

Sam rubbed his eyes and took a closer look at the large snowflakes falling around them. "It's snowing Letters, Lexius! Why is it snowing Letters?"

"Each of these beautiful flakes holds a Letter from the Alphabet, Sam. Each one is especially for you." Lexius glanced at his watch, looking a little concerned. "It's getting late" he muttered.

11

The Mountain, somewhat fierce looking due to its height, stood in the distance. Syia dazzled in the sky above its summit.

Sam started to fill with trepidation, as he viewed their destination point.

"Letter Mountain, Sam," said Lexius.

"Wow. It's huge. I didn't imagine it to be so big. Syia is so bright."

"Yes, they are quite something, aren't they!"

"So how do we get there? The sleigh has gone!"

"The sleigh is not needed here, Sam. For now, we will walk."

Through the village they strolled, sheltered by the cosy Blanket of Warmth and their warm snug boots.

They walked past a row of small but well-stocked shops, selling all types of goods such as food and kitchenware.

The last shop was an old-fashioned sweet shop, so it came as no surprise to see a large number of Goblin children hanging around outside with stuffed rosy cheeks and holding scrunched-up paper bags.

Sam felt a little conscious walking around with Goblins, after all it wasn't as if he did it regularly. Yet he could sense from their lack of interest in him, that they had become accustomed to human children dropping in unannounced.

Sam felt dusk creeping in around them and watched as the street lamps clicked on, one by one, just like they did back home. He guessed

the
shops
would soon
be closing for
the evening, ready
to begin again tomorrow.

Houses, built representing a Letter from the alphabet, lined both sides of the street. Crisp, frost-covered pathways led to small, bold coloured front doorways and streams of smoke swirled from brickwork chimney pots.

Sam's curiosity was getting the better of him. Tiptoeing up the icy path to a house that was the Letter I, he pressed his nose against a long narrow window and peered in.

His eyes followed the staircase up to see two excited Goblin children charge across the landing in their pyjamas, narrowly missing the stairs, waving their toothbrushes at each other in mock battle.

The pair continued on through the village. Lexius seemed anxious for them not to dawdle, so they picked up the pace.

As they walked towards the end of the High Street, the sweet aroma of toffee apples sprinkled with crushed roasted hazelnuts took over Sam's senses. His mouth started to water.

Looking to his right, Sam could see several Goblin children, clustered together in the small front garden of a house designed as the letter A.

There was a Goblin grandma standing in the doorway, holding a tray loaded with the delicious smelling apples.

Nostalgia filled his head. The smell reminded him of last summer's village fair, where he and Matty had played for hours without a care in the world, filling themselves up with candy floss and sticky apples.

Near the outskirts of the village, Sam saw a bustling bicycle park. A steam of older Goblin children were hurrying into the park, ready to grab a ride.

"Where are they all going to, Lexius? And why so many bicycles?"

"The Goblins use them to travel through the tunnel into Letter Mountain. Lots of the Goblin teenagers work inside the Mountain after school, or at the weekend. They help the Letter Goblin keep everything tidy and in order. The Great Library is housed in the Mountain too Sam. Everything you or anyone else will ever need to know is stored in the Great Library there."

"Let's grab a bike then and get going!" said Sam.

"No, lad, that would be too easy. Tonight is all about you challenging yourself. It's about you learning how you can achieve anything if you believe in yourself."

"Ohhh...," sighed Sam.

"We're heading that way!" Lexius lifted his paw and pointed in the opposite direction.

As they left the hustle and bustle of village life behind them, the pair stood for a moment, considering the snow-covered mountain that stood before them.

The ground beneath their feet started to shudder. The covering of freshly fallen snow fell away, revealing a long line of heavy-duty tracks.

Moments later, dressed in a glossy

pillar box red, the most splendid steam train came roaring over the heavy train tracks that protruded out from the vast mountainside.

"**We need this train Sam, and we need it now!**" howled Lexius. "It never stops when the land freezes over. The train despises the cold weather. No one rides it, there is nowhere to go."

The locomotive was travelling at great speed, and showed no loss of determination as it headed towards the final bend – it had no intention of stopping!

It struggled, it felt redundant and alone when Letter Land froze over. The elegant train would usually escort the Goblins up and down the mountain. In warmer times it would stop at all the tiny stations dotted along the way.

Goblins loved nothing more than to relax amongst the woodlands of the

Mountain
or swim in
its rivers.
**"Run for it,
Sam!"** bellowed
Lexius.
Sam clenched his
fists, held his breath... and
ran!
With hope pouring through
their veins and their legs on fire,
they lunged forwards as the last
carriage span round the bend.

"Jump, Sam!" Lexius growled the
command through his gritted teeth!

Sam jumped, as if his life depended
on it. A second or maybe two passed
before hands and paws grasped the
icy steel poles of the last carriage.

Filled with adrenaline and what little strength was left in their arms, boy and dog hauled themselves up and onto the train. They had made it!

The locomotive strove onwards and upwards on its relentless journey.

"We did it, Sam, we did it!" panted Lexius, his tongue hanging dry out of the side of his mouth.

Lexius had encountered the steam train many times over his years of working for the Letter Goblin, but he had become increasingly aware his age was catching up with him. Even in Letter Land, no one works for ever.

As the dog's furry chest laboured, Sam struggled momentarily with his own racing heart rate and tried to catch his icy breath.

"I'm fr-fr-freeeezing, Lexius, where did the Blanket of Warmth disappear to? I'm only wearing the boots you gave me and my summer pyjamas!"

His teeth sounded painful as they chattered beyond all control.

"The train is so powerful, Sam, that travelling at such great speed has caused the wind to extinguish the Blanket's power. We need to move quickly, we need to get you warmer. This chill won't be good for you at all."

Regaining a bit more composure, the pair stumbled their way through the train's empty compartments until they reached the halfway point.

Sam looked up and down the carriages. "So if the train NEVER stops, how do we...?" And then the penny dropped. "Surely not, no... we aren't just hurling ourselves off at the top of the mountain when the train passes there, **are we...?!** And I presume that's where the Letter Goblin lives?"

"Yes, Sam, the Letter Goblin lives near the top of the mountain..."

"This is madness. I know I wanted some fun, but really, is this possible?"

"Anything is possible, Sam. You just have to believe in yourself."

The carriage windows housed no glass, making it even colder as the bitter blistering wind whipped against Sam's defenceless pyjamas. His very pale-looking fingertips had started to lose all feeling, and attempting to blow life into his cupped hands had failed terribly.

Suddenly, a section of the decorative twinkly fairy lights that were attached to the top of all the carriages broke free, swaying frantically in the ferocious gale.

"I've got it!" Sam exclaimed. "Let's use the lights to swing out onto the mountain!"

"Err, could work...!"

The pair clambered up onto the latticed wooden seating. Sam couldn't help noticing how beautiful the deeply varnished seats looked and he felt a little guilty for standing on them with his boots on. His Mum would have gone mad.

Regardless of the harsh elements, the seats hadn't weathered, they looked brand new, cared for.

"Hope it doesn't snap, lad, I'm not the waif dog I used to be." Lexius looked doubtful as he patted his soft furry middle. "Too many sausage treats from my boss."

The pair had soon climbed up on to one of the train's shiny red window frames. Holding on tightly, wanting not to fall. Sam wrapped one hand and Lexius wrapped one paw around the fairy lights.

"Once we near the top of Letter Mountain, I will count to three, and on three we will swing out onto the mountain!" shouted Sam. "The snow looks fresh and deep, so our landing should be fairly soft.

"One... Twoo... Threeee!"

A few seconds later, Sam was wiping the snow from his face. He caught sight of Lexius and couldn't help but laugh at the little dog, who lay face up impersonating a snow angel.

The string of fairy lights lay broken yet still decorative as they continued to spark across Lexius's fluffy chest. It crossed Sam's mind that some multi-coloured tinsel and a Christmas fairy would have completed the look perfectly.

"Come on you funny dog, we're here at last!" giggled Sam.

The pair staggered onto their feet, regaining their composure. Beaming at each other they slapped a high five before collapsing back into the snow.

And then Sam felt his raw body begin to thaw. The Blanket of Warmth had reignited. It glowed around them once more.

12

Sitting back from the path, a very small, narrow yellow door sat proudly against the mountainside. Tied loosely to a dainty Goblin-shaped door knocker was a handwritten envelope. It was addressed to Sam.

He untied it and opened the envelope carefully.

"What does it say?" Lexius asked.

"Something about walking in the snow, but I can't say this word..." Sam held the note out to Lexius.

" 'Footprints'. It says we must walk through the **footprints** in the snow."

Sam was about to say "what

footprints?", when two lines of prints crunched out before his eyes in the snow. The pair walked over to stand where they began.

Sam tried to finish the Goblin note, but his

confidence had gone. But instead of asking Lexius to help him, he walked up to the yellow door, looking for its handle.

"How do we get inside the mountain, Lexius? The door doesn't have a handle to open it." Sam pushed firmly on the gleaming yellow panels. "It's stuck and there isn't a handle. What's the point of a door that has no handle and doesn't open?"

"The Letter Goblin is inviting you into her world, Sam," said Lexius.

"Well how do I get into her world, if I can't open the door? I couldn't fit through that teeny little door anyway, I'm far too big. I doubt you could wriggle through either!"

Lexius, feeling a little conscious of Sam's presumption, slumped down on his left shoulder.

It was the sort of slump his ancestors would have done just as they rolled in fox poop to disguise their scent from their prey. Casting his eyes towards his belly, he decided there was no harm in being a little cuddly.

Sam, feeling a pang of guilt for his forwardness, bent down to the silly dog.

"You're great just the way you are!" Sam said into Lexius's fluffy little ear. "Help me read the rest of the note please!"

"You can do it, Sam, it's only you and me here," said Lexius, still laying on his shoulder, his bottom poking up in the air.

Sam looked at the note and coughed, clearing his throat before he began: "This king only most wonderful..." And then he paused, sensing he was wrong.

"Take your time lad, try again." Lexius smiled encouragingly.

"Thinking only the most wonderful things...," read Sam.

"Well done Sam, but it's 'wonderful thoughts' not 'things'."

"TH words always come out wrong. It's like my eyes see the word but my mouth says whatever it wants," Sam explained, feeling more than a little awkward. "What should I think of, Lexius? I've never been asked to think about my thoughts before. How do I know what the right thoughts are?"

"Just whatever makes your insides warm, lad."

"And you, Lexius, what will you think of?"

Due to his natural instincts, sausages and tennis balls instantly popped into the little dog's head. He would struggle to decide between the two.

Lexius began chasing his tail in a rather strange manner.

Sam allowed the little dog a minute to get whatever it was out of his system. He then took control and gave the command "SIT!"

Following the instructions written on Sam's note left to him from the Letter Goblin, the pair began placing foot and paw carefully into the snow footprints.

"These footprints are your personal code into Letter Mountain, Sam. The pattern they have left in the snow, matches exactly the pattern on the sole of the snow boots you are wearing."

Sam lifted one foot up and then the other, studying the bottom of the boots Lexius had given him when they had landed on the planet.

He could see the zig-zag markings, the same as in the snow, but now he also noticed the capital letters, S and L which were his initials. Sam's surname was Larkin.

His date of birth was printed on them too: the fourth of September.

Sam walked the couple of yards beaming.

"Can I tell you what I'm thinking of Lexius, or will that stop things from working? You know, like you shouldn't tell anyone what you wish for, or it won't come true."

"Yes, you can tell me, Sam, it's not like making a wish."

"I would love to have another dog, Lexius. There's an animal shelter near to my home, I want to rescue one, give it a good home. It's all I think about," declared Sam.

Lexius was taken by surprise. His playful images were hijacked by Sam's thoughts, the idea of having a real home and someone like Sam to take care of him, a desire he had long since given up yearning for.

The caring canine had been turfed out of his 'forever home' many years ago once he had become too old to be any fun.

The little yellow door began bubbling and stretching in a very peculiar manner as they neared it. Sam gasped as he realised their bodies were also changing shape.

Lexius giggled as Sam's body bulged at the top and shrank at the bottom. Sam giggled as Lexius's face sank to his shoulders and his middle almost disappeared.

Just as Sam was about to ask what was happening, Lexius's furry paw grabbed his arm towards the door which promptly vacuumed them inside the mountain.

The pair stood just inside the bustling library. A vast collection of fiction and knowledge reached from floor to ceiling.

Reading was the one thing Sam feared the most, but that had never stopped him from being lured in by books with great illustrations and glorious colour. He always enjoyed snuggling up with his Mum at bedtime, listening and watching as his favourite Ninja stories unfolded on the pages.

You see, it wasn't that Sam didn't like books or stories, he just wanted to understand them better.

But those thin little pieces of paper, all covered with words, scared him.

Really scared him!

13

The huge colourful chamber
housed row upon row of drama,
knowledge and excitement. Sam
knew they were standing in what was
really just an elaborate library, but
somehow 'library' didn't seem fitting
enough for such a display.

Beyond the bookshelves, life seemed
a little hectic. Goblin girls and boys
were busy going about their business,
some more frantic than others.

Several of the older boys were
re-stocking the bookshelves. They
seemed to be having fun moving up,
down and across the shelves using
mechanical platforms. A group of
serious-looking girl Goblins had their

hands full, desperately trying to catch three large capital letters – S, T and O were running and jumping all over the place.

"Welcome, my dear Lexius. Welcome, Sam. Please come in!"

A grey-haired Goblin, much older than the rest, walked towards them.

"You made it Sam, how wonderful!" she said. "I'm Geraldine, the Letter Goblin. I have been waiting for you. Come, follow me."

The Letter Goblin led them to two very pretty chairs, gesturing Sam to sit next to her. Lexius jumped up onto an embroidered pouf cushion, circling and raking a few times before finally curling up and dozing off.

"Why are the Goblins chasing Letters, Mrs Goblin?" Sam asked.

"Oh Sam, please, call me Geri. As in Halliwell. You know, the excitable redhead in the Spice Girls!" chuckled the Letter Goblin.

Sam giggled as an amusing
chuckle-snort rippled around her gills,
turning her face quite a dramatic
shade of red. This of course clashed
dreadfully with the jolly Goblin's
green corduroy knee-length skirt.

The look on Sam's face was

enough to tell the jovial Librarian that he had absolutely no idea who she was referring to!

"My mother would say that 'Geraldine' loosely translates as 'Knowledgeable One'," Geri added with another snort and chuckle. "I'm sure she and I weren't born true Goblins. We've always had such a great sense of humour. Goblins are actually quite sombre creatures, Sam, and tend to take life rather too seriously I'm afraid. Goodness knows why – life here on Letter Mountain is so rewarding!"

"Geraldine... erm, Geri... Lexius thinks I'm Dyslexic and that is why I am struggling at school. Can you help me get better please? I really want to be able to read and write like my friends."

"Well... I can't make you 'better', Sam," said the Goblin slowly. "Because there is nothing wrong with you."

"Oh I see...," said Sam slowly. "I thought I would be able to read properly after tonight."

"I can't cure Dyslexia, Sam, but I can help you understand what is going on. A few changes here and there will make your school life easier, and the rest of your life will follow."

"But how do you know so much about Dyslexia?"

"Well, Goblins like myself are born to help children from your world. We are born under Syia, the brightest star in the sky whose powers automatically link us to a particular planet. Its power is so strong that it supports many other planets too.

"Here on Letter Mountain, Syia brings love and new beginnings to those who are struggling with Dyslexia. Syia sees how clever children like you are Sam. She knows Dyslexia is a highly creative strength and it will serve you well in life if you embrace it as a part of you.

"I was born many years ago, Sam, here on Letter Mountain. My father was the Letter Goblin, and upon his retirement, I was the obvious choice of successor to rule over the Mountain. I am Dyslexic Sam, just like my father was. He was a great leader, because he knew first hand (just as I do) how hard life can be when you don't find reading and writing easy.

"I really struggled as a young child, all the words would blur into one. There are many words I still have problems with even now, but that's OK. I have learnt how to deal with Dyslexia and accept it as a part of me.

"The Goblins need a leader, a bit like you have a Prime Minister. They trust that my own experiences with Dyslexia will help children from your world who struggle to read and write.

"Now I wouldn't class myself as overly clever, Sam, but I do have a lot of common sense. Common sense will help you greatly in life. I never dismiss something or someone as 'normal' or 'just going through a stage' And I always believe in love. Showing children love encourages their development and happiness."

Lexius's big hazel-brown eyes were gazing up at Sam and Sam felt his heart melt.

"It's about time he retired and settled down with a family of his own, I say, but he won't have it," said Geri. "Always on a mission to help other children, aren't you, Lexius? The old boy and I go back along way. He's a great dog, a really great pal. Lexius has brought many a girl and boy to visit us over the years, all with the same struggles as you. Haven't you, Lexius?"

Geri gave a nod to the scruffy-looking hound sprawled happily on the biggest cushion Sam was sure he would ever see.

"You've made a great friend right there, Sam" Geri smiled, shooting an affectionate wink at Lexius.

Kneeling down by the dog, she cupped his head with both hands and began scratching him softly behind both ears.

"So from a 'common sense' point of view, Geri...," Sam made the finger gesture he'd seen adults make when they were being a little sarcastic, "...what do you suggest I do?"

"Yes, right... Well don't just sit there you two, there's work to be done!"

14

Geri strode down the great Library Hall as Sam and Lexius followed.

"There are so many books here, Geri, have you read them all?"

"I have, Sam, every last one. Here in Letter Land we have a copy of every book that has ever been published. Your imagination and curiosity have the freedom to run wild here.

"We have books bursting with facts from history long, long ago, books that are busting their beautiful binders, crammed full of knowledge of the natural world. We keep these books safe so every child will have the chance to enjoy them. Whenever a new book is published, the original copy comes here for safekeeping. Books are very precious, Sam, they must be cared for properly."

"You didn't explain why the Goblins are chasing the Letters, Geri," said Sam

"Letters are little rascals and we think they can be taken over by a negative form of energy that even Syia cannot cancel out. Good often deals with a dose of bad, I'm afraid. I mean, Superman has to deal with Kryptonite and Luke Skywalker has to put up with Darth Vader!

"It is believed a dark force lives within the galaxy, Sam. We have to consider it is this dark energy that fuels the Letters into being naughty, but we don't know why. Letters are good, and yet can be highly mischievous when they turn their minds to it. And then their actions cause real problems for little ones like you. When they run around all over the place, they make it hard for you to focus.

"I mean, really, how can you read properly when the letter T keeps messing about on the page? Believe me, Sam, they think it's funny! We Goblins have a tiresome job. Using big nets to catch the Letters, we put them safely back where they belong – in the Alphabet Book.

"That way we try to keep them under control. It usually doesn't last for long, I'm afraid. But should they upset a child to a maximum of three times, their fate is then sealed! Our law clearly states that ALL NAUGHTY LETTERS may never return to the Alphabet Book, they must be taken to the Alpha Trash, a huge dustbin in the sky, a place of no return!

"You see, Sam, when a child doesn't receive the help they need, she or he starts to withdraw. Know that our planet bears the great weight of your sadness, Sam, and that is why Letter Land is forever freezing over.

"We see the endless sorrows that continually go unsupported with the children of your world. Supporting a child to read and write is a huge contribution to their future. It should be encouraged at all costs.

"Even though children develop these skills to different degrees, we Goblins believe that every child deserves the chance to achieve their skills without any heartache to themselves or their families!"

"But why don't you just erase all the bad Letters?" asked Sam. "That way all the sadness will go away."

"Oh come now, Sam, we can't just delete parts of the alphabet, can we?! The alphabet needs all of its twenty-six characters for you to write letters, emails, newspapers, text messages, signposts and so much more. You just need help in learning how to get along with the little monkeys!

"And, to make things even more frustrating, not every letter commonly associated with Dyslexia affects every Dyslexic boy or girl in the same way. Sam, we mustn't forget that the majority of people are not Dyslexic, so even if we could delete the Letters forever, that wouldn't be the right thing to do, now would it? Here on Letter Mountain we trust that one day ALL letters will be fuelled by Syia, not by the Dark Force!"

After accepting Geraldine was probably right, Sam dropped his gaze to the floor, lightly tapping the toe of one snow boot against the side of the other.

Sounding remarkably like a paddling pool, having the last puffs of air squeezed out of it at the end of summer, Sam sighed every last drop of air from his lungs, wishing SYIA would win that particular battle a little quicker!!

"Why do somethings have to be so difficult," he mumbled to himself.

15

Chaos had taken the Great Library by storm!

Long-legged T and S shaped letters ran round laughing loudly, whilst others in the form of H's and OO's stood blowing raspberries at each other and any Goblin passer-by.

"Sam, look out!" bellowed Lexius. A huge net came crashing down between them.

"Missed," grunted a wobbly Goblin. She had missed a capital B. Regaining her composure and picking up her enormous net, she ran off chasing the Letter with more determination than ever.

"Don't just stand there, Sam, grab your net!" Geri exclaimed. "Choose the Letters that hinder you most! Catch them, look them straight in the eye and tell them firmly that they no longer bother you. And Sam, you **must** believe it when you say it!"

"But Geri, they're so big compared to me!"

"Nonsense! You have to at least try, or you will never get anywhere. Now off you go!" shrilled the Goblin, pointing towards the cupboard under the spiral staircase. A sign on its door said 'NETS'.

Sam pushed the little door open and there in front of him, propped against the wall, was a long wooden pole with a large green net attached.

Sam gasped in surprise. "Geri, this net has my name stamped on it!" He instantly recognised his name, but was unsure of the small print that was carved into its pole.

"Yes, of course it does, Sam," said

Geri. "As I told you, we've been waiting for you."

"But what do the other words mean? It says something about getting a 'bear'! Why do I need a bear?" Sam asked.

"Take another look," said Geri. "It doesn't say **bear**, it says **bears**."

"What does **bears** mean, Geri?"

"Well, in this case it means 'to hold'. The net holds your name Sam, so its duty is to help you win your battle."

" 'Whoever's name the net bears, its honour is to serve'," Sam read more confidently this time.

"Yes, brilliant, that's exactly what it says, well done Sam!"

Sam looked at Geri and smiled.

The Goblin caught the look in Sam's eyes. The look that said, You understand me.

Geri didn't want to linger, she knew Sam's time was staring to run out.

She consciously changed her tone.

"Now will you please get on with the job! I don't need to remind you young man that you don't have all night!"

16

From the corner of his right eye, two Letters in particular caught Sam's attention. And they were going in the Alpha Trash!

Running up the staircase were the Letters T and H. These were two naughty Letters that especially gave Sam trouble on a daily basis. Constantly perched on his shoulder, they laughed at him when he couldn't recognise words like **his** and **this**.

Of course he understood that locking his enemies in a book or throwing them in the Alpha Trash wasn't going to stop him being Dyslexic, but for some reason he was starting to feel a little confident.

Sam made a pact with himself.

If he caught these Letters and dealt with them, he would ask his Mum to try again to get him help at school. He also hoped people would be more understanding of his difficulties.

In fact, Sam was beginning to think that by standing up for himself he could help other struggling children to be recognised.

The Letters seemed as twisted as the staircase. They stood laughing at him from the top step. Sam desperately wanted to catch the wayward offenders and let them know their days of raining havoc on him were over.

With a fierce yell, he charged up the staircase... Just a moment too late!

His heart sank as he passed the duo riding the highly varnished banister on a very slippery descent.

"No!" Sam shouted. "You come back here, right now!"

Sam threw himself onto the banister, as the T and H hurtled down towards Lexius and Geri, who stood staring up in amazement.

"Go on lad, get 'em!" barked Lexius. The excitement triggered him to chase his tail again, howling with encouragement.

Nearing the bottom of the staircase the Letter T lost its footing, falling sideways.

The top of the T became entwined with the bar of the Letter H, causing the meddlesome pair to lose their balance, crashing down the last few feet, landing at the foot of the staircase in a tangled heap.

As he whizzed down towards them, Sam saw his chance and took it. "Keep calm and focus," he told himself. "Keep calm and focus."

He kept repeating the mantra then

took a deep breath just as he felt his bottom leave the banister.

He too had lift-off, but unlike those naughty letters, Sam descended with more grace and sailed through the air straight towards the Letters.

Distracted whilst bickering over

whose fault it was that they were in this mess, both the Letters failed to notice Sam about to land on top of them.

After using them as a very uncomfortable landing pad, Sam jumped up and captured them in his net.

"Gotcha!" he yelled.

"Howwwt-standing!" howled Lexius.

"**Great show!**" bellowed Geri.

The squabbling letters continued fighting with each other for a minute or so longer before realising they had been captured.

After pulling at the netting in disbelief, the letter T poked its tongue out at Sam, whilst the letter H rolled its eyes and stamped its feet.

"Where's the Alpha Book, Geri? Let's get them in there!" gasped Sam as he wrapped the Letters firmly in the net.

"Oh no, lad, those two reprobates can't be returned to the Alpha Book. They have caused far too much trouble on more than one occasion! You need the Alpha Trash for them and that's in the Upper Library. Use the lift, it will save you valuable time."

Geri pointed to the far side of the room, waving her arm back and forth through the air as if directing a Boeing 747 to take off.

"The lift will open right outside the Upper Library door. Be sure to ask for Squiggles, he's my Managing Letter Librarian. Tell him you wish to use the **Naughty Letters Alpha Trash**, otherwise known as **N-LAT**. Squiggles will help you use the Letter hoist, as believe me it's quite a wrench to haul them up!"

"But what if the Letters escape, what shall I do? I'm running out of time," asked Sam, now worried.

"They won't, they can't! Once the child they are bothering has caught them and stood up to them, their game is over. You have taken control, Sam."

Geri tried to settle Sam's concern with a warm smile and a thumbs up.

"Of course reading and writing will always have their challenges," she said. "But they won't bother you in the way they did. The Letters' battle with you has been fought and you've won!

"I suppose what I'm trying to say is: understanding more of your learning difficulties will naturally boost your confidence when you return home. You need more time and understanding at school, Sam. But don't worry, it will happen. They are a kind bunch there, it's just that they just lost you in the crowd.

"You can have stories to read where the words are more spaced out and the font is bigger or darker. Some children find putting see-through coloured plastic sheets over the pages really helps. And there are Reader Pens too, these days! They are amazing – you scan over the words or sentences you are trying to read and they read it out aloud to you. How brilliant is that!"

"So all these things can help me read better, Geri?"

"Yes my lovely, but first you must start by telling your Teacher you are Dyslexic, Sam, and then…"

Sam heaved a dispirited sigh at the Letter Goblin's words, and his whole body slumped.

"I can't just say, 'Good morning, Miss, how was your weekend? Mine was crazy. A sneezing dog arrived from an unknown planet. He sat on the end of my bed and told me I am Dyslexic. His name is Dog-Lexius. He took me in a Flying

Water Bowl to see Geraldine the Letter Goblin. Who, by the way, compares herself to a lady in a group that has something to do with spice? She had me chasing letters around!' "

"Ahh, um...," muttered the Goblin, tapping her index finger against her temple.

"My Teacher thinks I'm hard work as it is," Sam continued, "so this will do me absolutely no favours with her at all, trust me. I may as well quit school for good."

"Well, yes, I can see your point. But don't worry, we just have to box a bit clever about that," said Geri. "I have a drawer of 'Certified Dyslexic' certificates in my office. Whilst you are sorting out those naughty Letters upstairs, I will send Lexius to fetch your Certificate."

"So what happens when I get these Letters up to the Alpha Trash?"

"Well, Sam it's not the simplest of tasks, as the Letters are rather large as you know."

Sam was now listening carefully. Geri had his full attention. He was not going to fail.

"Take your time," Geri instructed. "The opening the letters must drop through is not as big as you may presume. Align each letter accurately over the Alpha Trash. Only when you are sure that each Letter will fall straight through, with no catching or sticking to the sides, do you carefully release the hoist's great claw, releasing the character."

Sam didn't utter a word, his head was full of letters, trash cans and big metal claws.

"Once the offender has passed through the opening, into the atmosphere, pull the lid down and replace the padlock. But a word of warning, lad, you must take great care not to topple in. The Alpha Trash is way mightier than you can imagine."

"Once something goes in, there's absolutely no way of return. The Backdraft Dampening System is designed to withstand the malodorous whiff created by the Letters as they depart from Letter Land (probably got something to do with what they ate for dinner, I suspect – Letters fuelled by a Dark Force, should that be what the problem is, have dreadful eating habits).

"But we're not littering the atmosphere with our unwanted waste, Sam. The Letters are composed of rice-paper, sugar and bicarbonate of soda. A little like some of your world's edible cake decorations.

"And so the moment they enter the force field surrounding Letter Land, they fizzle like a popsicle would on your tongue, dissolving pretty much instantly!"

"Oh...," was all Sam could muster up. It was all rather a lot to take in.

"I mean, if more things could be made this way it would certainly help with the cosmic issue of environmental waste, don't you think lad?"

Geri glanced sideways rather briskly, before admitting: "The Alpha Trash is also a good way to 'lose' my Auntie Dorothy's handmade Christmas jumpers! She tends to knit them out of the same stuff and believe me, Sam, they can be extremely itchy, as I'm sure you can imagine!"

Sam, finding her confession quite funny patted Geri on the arm, before heading off towards the lift dragging the Letters with both hands behind him.

Pushing the UP button on the wall,

he waited a couple of seconds for the lift to arrive.

In the distance, he could hear the Letter Goblin chuckling to herself over her Christmas jumper confession, when the lift doors slid open.

Sam heaved the hefty Letters inside, closed the doors and pressed UP!

17

"Hello, is anyone here? Geri sent me to find Squiggles."

An array of tiny Goblin faces shot up like characters in a pop-up book.

Sam froze, reluctant to move any further. Twenty pairs of green, doe-like eyes rested upon him.

"Come now, everyone, back to your revision, exams start next week!" A voice with a tone of authority rang out to break the silence.

From behind a bookshelf a face appeared, much younger than the voice had led Sam to believe.

"Hello, Sam!"

"Squiggles?"

"Yes, that's me. Please let me help you with those two Letters."

"They're rather difficult."

"It will be my pleasure, Sam!" said the friendly Managing Letter Librarian.

Sam grabbed the net and with Squiggles' help he dragged the Letters over to a rectangular-shaped pillar that stood in a statuesque manner in the centre of the room.

A magnificent wooden ladder, crimson in colour, lay idle against its side. Sam instantly recalled the bark of the Wanna-Wanna Tree growing deep in the forest.

Staring up toward its pinnacle, he could just make out the Alpha Trash's outer rim.

"Start climbing the ladder whilst I fetch the hoist," Squiggles told him.

The most brain-scraping, eyebrow-raising sound pierced the room, disrupting the student Goblins once again. As Squiggles continued pushing the squeaky hoist towards Sam, he made a note to himself to see to its three huge wheels, which desperately needed oiling.

Once at the summit, Sam could see the Alpha Trash in all its enormity. There was a large padlock keeping the lid shut tight. To the side of the pillar hung a shiny silver key, dangling silently off an even shinier silver hook.

"Let's do this!" Sam shouted down to Squiggles. As he did so, he saw that the noise had disturbed the Goblins again and he couldn't help asking: "What are they revising for, Squiggles?"

"The production of Letter Flakes and the day-to-day running of the Great Library."

" 'Letter Flakes'?"

"They cover the mountainside, you would have walked in them earlier.

Do you remember it snowing when you arrived?"

"Yes, I do remember. Are the Letter Flakes important?"

"They are extremely important. When a child struggles and Letter Land starts to freeze, it snows very hard at first. We harvest the Snow Flakes as quickly as possible and reproduce each one with a handmade Letter from the Alphabet.

"The Flakes only carry meaning for each individual child who comes to our world. Each Letter Flake is coated with Alpha Dust before it's blasted back out over the mountain. All the Letters laying over the Letter Mountain today are unique to you, Sam."

"So what's Alpha Dust then?" Sam asked, even more intrigued.

"It's the most magical property we possess. It has the potential to change a child's world. From the moment you stand on the snow-covered mountain, its energy will travel through your body to help you to complete your quest. Its strength will live within you until you no longer need it.

"Alpha Dust will help your Mum and Teachers understand your struggles. The Certificate that Geri will give you is glazed with Alpha Dust, so the moment your Mum and Teachers touch the paper it will appear to them as an original diagnosis of Dyslexia from your own world. Our aim is for you to receive the help and support you deserve, Sam."

"Wow, so much goes on here! May I see the Letter Flakes being made?"

"Yes, if there's enough time, but you need to deal will these two Letters first!"

Squiggles finished loading the Letter T onto the hoist. Once he was happy it was hooked securely, he pulled down hard on the rope. Squiggles joined Sam at the top of the ladder to help him heave the Letter up.

Once it reached the top, Sam wrapped the rope securely around the brass hook and climbed up a little further to fetch the key. Sam put it inside the padlock, and turned it anti-clockwise. The lock released with more ease than he would have guessed.

The hefty lid flew open, crashing back onto its hinge with a clang, making Sam jump.

Resting his palms on the edge of the Trash Can, he dared himself a glimpse over the edge. He had momentarily lost sight of Geri's warning, telling of how disastrous it would be if he fell into the bin. A feisty pull of air drew downwards, tugging at his forehead and cheeks.

His eyes had felt the drag too, but thankfully they were still in his head.

That was more than enough to curb Sam's curiosity and remind him that he **really** wanted to see his Mum again sometime soon!

Sam lent over to the hoist, taking hold of the strap that restrained his arch enemy.

It's time I put you where you belong, he thought to himself.

18

Sam carefully guided the hoist's tray over the top of the Trash Can. When all seemed level, he caught hold of the mechanical claw, dragging it over his tormentor.

A metal lever to work the claw sat attached to the same wooden post as the key. Sam pushed and held it in until the claw sat close above its prey.

The arrows on the post gave all the instructions he needed to work the claw. Sam used both hands to pull the lever out and upwards, enabling the basic yet impressive device to open wide.

Observing the claw for just a

moment longer, he allowed his overactive imagination to get carried away by conjuring visions of his dentist using something similar to extract a troublesome tooth!

Sam felt a sharp pain stab at his jaw causing him to wince. Cupping his jaw with his left palm, he remembered his up and coming dental appointment...

With everything in place, Sam just needed to close the claw. He pulled the lever hard to the left, allowing the huge steel pincers to clench firmly around the huge T.

All he needed to do now was to remove the tray before releasing the claw.

Feeling relieved to have got this far, Sam took caution in sliding the tray out and to the right of the T, which was now left dangling in mid air.

Sam couldn't quite bring himself to

feel victorious whilst his opponent
lay there helpless, surrendering to its
fate. Breathing deeply and feeling a
little giddy, his head was suddenly
filled with the sound of Squiggles's
shouting up at him.

"Brilliant, Sam! I will start getting the Letter H ready." Squiggles guided the tray back down and loaded up the next offender. "What are you waiting for, Sam? Release the claw!"

Sam hesitated. Somehow things didn't seem quite the same now that his enemy lay submissive in front of him.

"Will the Letter suffer, Squiggles? Will it hurt when it enters the galaxy?"

"Oh no, Sam, it won't feel anything, I promise. Letters are only produced from rice paper and powered by gas. No sympathy, Sam! It's only a Letter, and Letters don't have feelings. All this one has is just bad gas and negative energy!!"

Squiggles hoped his explanation would reassure the boy that everything was OK, and this is how life is on Letter Mountain.

Clearing his throat, Sam pushed

the lever to the right, prompting the claw to open. His oppressor dropped like a stone!

An almighty drag of air sucked Sam chest first against the side of the Trash Can. His hair followed, anchored down only by the grace of its youthful roots.

Squiggles had helped him be free of the great burden that had sat on his shoulders for too long.

He hoped that he would have time to deal with the Letter B, but for now the Letter H was about to follow the T – and although it was not an elementary task, Sam knew he had won this particular battle!

19

Waiting outside the Library doors, Sam tried to take in what had just happened. Squiggles had hung back to help a couple of his younger student Goblins who had some queries about their studies. Like Sam, they didn't find reading and writing easy.

Squiggles caught up with Sam just as the lift arrived. Stepping in, the two travelled to the very top floor of the Library.

Squiggles took down two protective suits, handing the larger to Sam. Once they were sealed up in their suits, the Managing Letter Librarian swiped a metal key card through the card reader that was sitting neatly on the wall.

"The suits are designed to protect us from the sub-zero temperatures within the room," Squiggles explained. "It is of great importance that we mimic the outside temperature to stop the Snow Flakes from melting.

"The Goblins wear special gloves to protect the flakes and their hands whilst they work. Each pair of gloves are extremely thin. They are designed with a micro layer inside that houses a small vacuum of heat to keep their hands from seizing up. The outer layer of the glove is coated in a unique technology that regulates at a very chilly minus one degree! Once each Flake has had a Letter attached to its centre, it is ready to be redistributed over the mountain."

"So is this it?" frowned Sam.

"This is it!" said Squiggles.

"I thought it would be all wheels and cogs. I thought there would be a merry-go-round of noisy machinery."

"Ahh yes, indeed you would, Sam," laughed Squiggles. "But it is surprising how little we need here to complete our work. Walk with me Sam, let me explain."

Sam walked with Squiggles to the corner of the room, where a large glass receptacle sat protruding from the wall.

"A huge vacuum lies within this wall, Sam. It draws the snow laying on the mountainside into this cylinder. A bit like a vacuum cleaner sucking up dirt off your kitchen floor.

"The snow then slides slowly down the zig-zag pipework until it reaches the Goblins, who work tirelessly, separating each of the frosty Flakes before fusing each one individually to a delicately hand-carved Letter, using

just a single frost stitch.

"The Letter Flakes are carved
from ice, by our own highly skilled
Ice Artists. Only when the Goblins
are happy that the two have bonded

perfectly, are the Flakes then placed on the frozen glass conveyor belt. When they reach the top, they flutter down into this, we call it a Snowcain-O."

Squiggles pointed to another glass cylinder, where lots of snowflakes were puffing up and floating around. Sam thought it looked sort of pretty.

"We call it a Snowcain-O because it eventually erupts just like a volcano blasting out hot lava! A gentle flow of cold air keeps the Letter Flakes aloft and the Alpha Dust circulating. Only when the cylinder is holding exactly **one thousand** dust-covered Letter Flakes will it erupt!

"Huh-huh-huh CHOOO!!"

Sam and Squiggles turned to see Lexius standing just behind them.

"Thought I would wander up to see how you are getting on Sam," sniffed the little dog inquisitively.

"I'm having a great time Lexius!"

"Cool, I will be downstairs with Geri when you've finished here with Squiggles." Lexius winked at Squiggles before trotting back out of the **chilly** room.

"Can you see that box displaying digital numbers?" Squiggles pointed to the red counter attached to the back of the cylinder.

"Err, yes…," replied Sam, trying to take it all in.

"Well, that counter tells us exactly how many Flakes are in the drum at any one time. It is so sensitive, it can detect the weight of every dainty flake."

"Squiggles, this place is crazy!" beamed Sam. "Does anything ever go wrong?"

"Ha ha!" laughed Squiggles. "No, thankfully. Although we did have a drama a couple of years ago when the only Letter produced all day was Z!"

He laughed out loud again, recalling that frightful day. "I had an appointment on your planet, Sam. I left a voicemail for Zufus, one of our more senior Goblins, explaining my wishes for the day's work ahead. I asked him to make sure the Goblins had **made their beds**, and to produce **two hundred Zs before my return. Our Z stock was running a little low, and I do like the Letter Chiller to be kept topped up.**

Unfortunately, a relatively young T-Tauri star had exploded somewhere in the galaxy a couple of days before. The hurricane-type winds created by an event like that always cause some damage to our mobile phone connection. And that's why Zufus misheard the broken crackly message and instructed the Goblins to stop what they were doing and produce **'lots of Z's',** two thousand Z's, to be precise!"

Sam gulped, "WOW, that's a lot of Z's!"

"Instead of checking the Letter Chiller first, or calling me back on our super charged Snow-Line, which is like a back-up generator in your world, he just presumed we had run too low, and without a sufficient amount of Z's, all publications of the great children's books 'Zig-Zagging Zara' and 'Who Zapped Zany?' would have to be put on hold!"

"OMG!" said Sam. "I love those stories, we have them in the school library. They have awesome pictures too!"

"I had left Letter Land early that morning, journeying down the Rainbow Skelter. The Skelter is our fastest route to your planet, where I wanted to oversee Molly, a girl about the same age as you, Sam.

"She was so sad, she was really

struggling to read and write. Poor Molly, she lacked the confidence to tell anyone about how she was feeling at school. Molly had become rather quiet over the months that led up to my visit, and it had been presumed that she just hadn't settled well in her new school year.

"You see, Sam, girls suffering with Dyslexia often tend to react differently to boys. Where boys tend to become rather loud, or over-busy to distract from what they can't do, many girls have a tendency to withdraw instead.

"Now we knew about Molly because Lexius had woken up the morning before with a cold nose. Dogs have great senses in their noses. Obviously food odours will send Lexius scatty, but he also has the ability to sniff out degrees of climate change."

"Gosh, Lexius didn't tell me that!"

Sam thought how awesome that would be.

"When Lexius has a chilly nose, it's our first indication that a child is withdrawing and Letter Land is beginning to freeze over again."

"Did Molly come to Letter Land, Squiggles?"

"She did. And believe me, she is happy and doing well at school now. And that's all down to her Teachers giving her the extra help she needs."

"So what happened with Zufus?" Sam was intrigued to hear the end of the drama.

"Well, I arrived back just as the Snowcain-O started bubbling, ready to erupt! I knew it had to be for the **second** time that day, as I immediately realised there were already Z's crunching beneath my feet. I spotted that all the Letters in the cylinder were **more Z's!** But by then it was far too late. **Another**

one thousand Z's burst out of the Snowcain-O ready to settle over the Mountain!"

"Was Zufus in trouble?"

"Oh no, I couldn't be cross with him! It was just a silly mistake. But he does, however, always double check with me first now via the Snow-Line if our mobile phone connection is weak," said Squiggles, with a cheeky wink.

"Squiggles, look!" Sam pointed at the monitor behind the Goblin.

Squiggles turned to see the sum of nine hundred and ninety-nine flashing on the monitor.

"Can I watch the Snowcain-O erupt? Please, please can I?"

"Of course. But to view this spectacular display we do need to be outside Sam. That's where all the Goblins' hard work can really be appreciated!"

Squiggles steered Sam rather

hastily towards the door.

Sam turned, looking back over his shoulder. **One thousand** angelic flakes were now bubbling up and down in sizeable, splendid puffs within the cylinder.

The room became a hive of excitement. Goblin folk from every corner rushed to exit the room.

"Hurry Sam, encouraged Squiggles. The letters in the Snowcain-O are ready to explode out of the cylinder. Once they settle, you will be able to witness our great Syia Star shining at her brightest! Her strength will fill the new letters with **COURAGE, STRENGTH** and **DETERMINATION.**

"The Woodpecker will sense another child will soon be on their way to Letter Mountain and the Huskies will be ready for action! That's how Letter Mountain works Sam.

A horn sounded, followed by a

triumphant cheer that rose up into the frosty air.

One thousand spectacular Letter Flakes burst free, momentarily blocking out the skyline. Syia exploded with light, her full strength beaming-out the most vivid rays of white light. Sam and the Goblins took a step backwards, their hands shielding their eyes from Syia's brilliance. These flakes were to be the last burst of energy surrounding Sam's adventure on Letter Mountain.

After the last Flake had settled, the Goblins, content with their latest achievement, turned back to go inside the Mountain and flowed towards the dining hall. It was time for a well deserved break. It was time for a cup of tea!

20

Sam took the lift back down to the ground floor. The door pinged open and Sam spotted Geri and Lexius sitting at the far side of the room.

They appeared to be deep in conversation. Sam walked towards them, overhearing something about a "piñata". He decided to butt in!

"Why would I need a piñata, Geri?" Sam quizzed, leaning over Lexius's shoulder.

"It's not quite 'piñata' as you know it, lad!" Geri explained.

Lexius, aware Sam now only had thirty-three minutes remaining before the last of the three rings disappeared, winked at the Letter Goblin and took over.

"We think of it more as a Memory Pool," the dog explained. "Your challenge, should you feel comfortable accepting it, is to break its shell, releasing its contents. Every Memory Pool is unique. Sam, your time here is nearly up, but you haven't confronted your history regarding school life and you really should deal with the Letters B and D before you leave."

"What do I need to do?"

"You have to hit the Memory Pool Piñata with as much force as possible, weakening its shell. Not an easy task – the shell is coated with a tough membrane because Memory Pools can be very stressful emotionally. You will relive things from your past that you have tried to hide from. You should prepare yourself now, for what you are about to see."

"OK," said Sam. "I'm a tough cookie, I can do it."

Lexius stood up, engaged in a yogic slow motion, upward and downward dog to stretch out and ease his ageing spine, before scratching under his left armpit and trotting towards the door.

Geri, on the other hand, stayed where she was.

"Come on, Geri, I need you too!" said Sam. "I know I just said I can do this Memory Pool thing, but only with you two with me. I'm only nine years old!"

"Sam, this is where we say our goodbyes," the Letter Goblin smiled. "You don't need me now. I create these obstacles as a way for you to challenge yourself. A way for you to see you are capable of achieving anything.

"Don't let some silly Letters rule your life! Many wonderful children have come to visit me over the years, and many have gone on to achieve above and beyond what they ever thought possible. They, like you, just needed Letter Land's helping hand.

"All of the children who have spent time here on Letter Mountain have blossomed beautifully, going forwards in their lives with confidence. Not everyone can read and write perfectly, Sam. But NOT being scared to be seen as a little different makes the world a better place. It gives others hope.

"Who knows what lies ahead for you? You may become an entrepreneur, building businesses that supply many other people with jobs and income to support their lives and families. You have expressed a love of baking and who knows where that may take you?

There are brilliant chefs with inspiring skills, and although some may struggle with literacy, they have gone on to feed our imaginations and fill our dinner tables with their tasty delights. Brilliant recipe books have been written and sold, yet the authors would have needed to embrace the help of others and technology in order to write them.

"So, Sam, you just need to believe in yourself and the rest in time will follow."

Sam fought to hold back the tears he felt brewing. His Mum always told him that everything would work out in the end if he just believed in himself more. Now he really, truly believed that it would all eventually be OK.

"I will never forget what all of you have all done for me, Geri," he managed finally to say. "Keep doing what you do and don't ever leave us children alone!"

Sam ran to the Letter Goblin, his heart exploded, his tears fell.

21

Geraldine had already instructed the Goblins to hang Sam's Memory Pool alongside the Rainbow Skelter.

Time was running out for the young boy on Letter Mountain. His journey this evening had taken longer than it should.

By now the two purple rings would be radiating at full strength, and he needed all the energy they had to power the Flying Water Bowl back to his home and back to his Mum.

Lexius's head hung low, an aching feeling had hijacked his heart.

The little dog found it hard to look Sam in the eye. He was worried that the boy would see his true need to be loved. He wished desperately to save them both the stomach-curdling wrench that came with goodbyes.

Lexius had escorted so many children to Letter Mountain, caring for them all dearly, but this felt different.

Lexius believed he and Sam were destined to meet, and not just because of Dyslexia. Sam was Lexius's forever home!

Geraldine had been more than just his best friend. It was Geri who had rescued him from the abandoned animal shelter so many years ago. Lexius trusted she would find a suitable successor, but because this was all he had known for so long, would he really fit back into domestic life?

He was scared, yes, but he knew that, unlike his previous family, Sam would never cast him aside once he became too old to chase a ball.

Aware that the Memory Pool Piñata was still hanging, unbroken, waiting, the little dog coughed a couple of times, clearing his throat.

Lexius spoke to the floor, his eyes heavy with emotion: "Throughout your school life many things have been considered the cause of your struggles, Sam...

—He's naughty!

—He's one of the eldest in the year!

—He's bored!

—He's just playing up for attention!

"It would seem that no one ever considered the possibility that you just couldn't put down on paper what was being asked of you. But Letter Land understands that brains work differently and that every child is an individual.

"Unfortunately, Sam, people can be scared or frustrated by things that don't present as normal. People can think it may take up too much time to deal with an individual or the minority, and sadly it costs extra money that schools just don't have.

"Although it is commonly reported that Dyslexia cannot be conclusive until a child is roughly eight years old, many children just like yourself will already be displaying the related traits from a much younger age."

For the first time since all this started, from the moment he heard Lexius sneeze at the end of his bed, Sam wanted to go home. He wanted his Mum!

22

"Your Memory Pool Piñata is full of information that Squiggles has gathered about you since your school life began."

"Give me the stick please, Lexius, I want to get this done," said Sam simply, broadening his shoulders. His stern tone was more to hide his feelings for Lexius rather than what the Memory Pool may hold.

The scruffy little dog extended his paw, offering Sam the Wanna-Wanna Stick. Sam wrapped his hand around the opposite end of the crimson wood.

Lexius' lips pulled back over his teeth, as if he were about to attack the stick!

"Huh-huh-huh-**choooo!**" A wet blob of doggy snot landed on Sam's pyjama sleeve!

"It's the du... "

"I know, you daft dog, it's the dust!" Sam grinned. "Come home with me Lexius, when all this is done. Please, come home with me."

"I... I can't, Sam. Others need me."

"But Geri said you should think of retiring, so why not now? Come to live with me. My Mum won't mind. I will always look after you, I promise." Sam's voice started to wobble.

Lexius dropped his gaze. Stepping back, he left Sam to complete his last task.

23

The Memory Pool Piñata hung in the shape of a capital B and D, their spines moulded together. Sam studied it carefully, planning which angle of attack would be the most effective – he had no time to waste!

Raising his arms over his head, Sam brought the Wanna-Wanna Stick down hard, making no impression on the burly B. The exasperating Letter was defiant, acknowledging yet again its role to be awkward.

Again and again Sam brought down the crimson stick, finding more power with every strike.

"Seven, whack! Eight, whack!" he counted out loud.

Strike number nine came crashing down. A small emission of light escaped from the Letters' base.

"Ten, whack! Eleven!"

Sam worked on, grunting like a Wimbledon finalist. Twelve, thirteen, fourteen... and then suddenly something broke free!

Gripping the Wanna-Wanna Stick in his hand, Sam suddenly saw a string of several blue Vapour-like visions drifting above his head.

"See that one there," Sam pointed to a ghost-like Vapour, imaging a boy holding a bird's nest. "That was me in Reception year. I wanted so desperately to take that nest to school for Show and Tell. But my Teacher looked sceptical as I explained how the birds had used some of my dog's bedding to enhance their accommodation.

"A few days before, a wind had picked up just as my Mum decided to spring-clean our dog's bed. We always knew when Harvey was in a grumpy mood because he would chew pieces off his blanket! And it was those nibbled little pieces of fleece that the birds had gathered to make a cosy home.

"That afternoon, at home time, my Teacher gave my Mum her views on my storytelling. Mum soon put her right though, she stood up for me.

She explained that my account of events was accurate.

"That Teacher never did like me, and I don't think she liked my Mum much either. I was only five, Lexius. I was so excited that morning, carrying the delicate little nest to school, but I walked home sad and confused.

"Mum didn't like the way my Teacher always rolled her eyes to the ceiling, shattering my enthusiasm across the doorway of the classroom. Mum joked that the Teacher was looking up to the heavens for help, wishing they would exchange me for a different pupil.

"But my Mum wished for a spell that would soften my Teacher's judgemental manner."

24

Confident he had dealt with the first Vapour, Sam cast his attention to another. He laughed, pointing at a grid shape floating above.

And then he sighed. "Sticker charts...

"If only my Teacher knew how ambitious these are for me. Struggling to concentrate on things that don't interest me, and having the extra pressure of having to read or write about them, just to get a sticker and reward really is a nightmare for me.

"If my brain can't decode what my Teacher has been talking about, then I can't write about it, can I?

Sometimes, I feel that if I can manage to get the stickers, she can at least show my Mum something positive about me?"

"I know Sam," said Lexius, breaking in to Sam's thoughts. " I wish people could just realise that no amount of stickers will make a child's brain work differently."

Attached to this particular Vapour hung a picture of Sam's Mum. She was crying. Seeing his Mum upset sparked a sudden anger inside him.

Swinging the Wanna-Wanna Stick above his head, he froze for a few seconds, closing his eyes for just a little longer than intended. Etched within the darkness of his eyelids lay the outline of his Mum, sitting cross-legged on their kitchen floor, all his sticker charts spread out before her.

"When you are different, you're just a problem," he thought. "I want to go home!" Whack! "I want to go home! **I want toooo...!**"

"Sam! Stop! Look up!" shouted Lexius.

The steadfast Letters had collapsed. He had broken their bond!

Sam sank to his knees, exhausted.

Two more Vapours floated out from the piñata, following Sam down to the ground.

The light blue, swirly Vapours were Sam's most treasured memories.

They drifted softly in the air before wrapping themselves adoringly around their grandson.

Losing both his Granddads, the first in Reception Year, the second in Year 1, had been a blow in many ways.

No matter what was going on in his school life, spending time with these two amazing characters helped make things a little easier somehow. Both had the ability to hold his attention when most others failed.

Sam was wrapped in his happiest memories. He laughed as he watched himself fighting with Grandad Biscuit's hedgerow, prodding it with his little plastic sword, totally unaware of the wasps nest hidden inside.

The buzzing pirates were not best pleased with 'Captain Sam, Ruler of the Seven Seas' poking at their home, so they had swiftly taken charge. Sam had no other option other than to make a very hasty retreat!

Captain Sam ran crying across the patio, through the kitchen and up the hallway to Grandad Biscuit, who brought out the best treasure chest in the world, his biscuit tin! A couple of chocolate digestives later, all was as it should be and no one had been made to walk the plank.

Grandad H (a.k.a. Harold), had a heart of gold and a generous personality. This 'H' (unlike the Letter H) always made him laugh. Sam twisted from side to side to watch and remember the irreplaceable times he had sat tucked up under his Grandad's arm, listening wide-eyed to the most ridiculous of yarns. Stories as wide, as they were long. Stories that only a true storyteller could fashion.

Letter Mountain may have helped Sam deal with the Letter H, leaving his future looking so much brighter, but things would never be quite the same without the other H and there was nothing Sam could do to change that.

From the other side of the Rainbow Skelter Room, Lexius watched the smile that this memory spread across Sam's face. A smile so warm and wide that lifted the boy's spirits and brightened his eyes like diamonds.

25

Lexius glanced at his watch. Only four minutes remained! Once the hands hit 5 a.m., the Rainbow Skelter would burst into life.

"**Sam!**" screamed Lexius. "It's almost **5 a.m.! Hurry!**"

Lexius scrabbled up to the Rainbow Super-Slide, punching Sam's home address into the navigation system as fast as his paws would allow.

Sam was now immersed in the last of his Vapours and he hadn't detected the urgency in Lexius' voice.

His memories had taken him back to school, watching as child after child reaped the rewards of their labours in class.

Admittedly, many of his classmates worked hard at school, not everything was as easy as 1-2-3 for them either, but being able to read and understand still gave them an advantage. And for those who found learning fun and a breeze, praise came naturally.

Sam however just wanted to be recognised for **something**.

His nemesis floated in front of his face! The little disc of shiny metal, the one designed to tell the world how great your handwriting is. The coveted treasure Sam never received.

Sam winced. Just the thought triggered the uncomfortable pain he felt from holding his pen in class.

Schools love a badge and the children who wear them, all in a row like military recognition. But what did they know about being brave? What did they know about getting up every morning just to go into battle?

Sam was busy in his head, designing a badge for all those children like him who went to school everyday regardless of their struggles.

A badge for those who tried their best when everyone around them seemed to understand, but they didn't.

A great big badge telling everyone how hard school is, but you still made it in, and you ARE trying your best!

Sam stood there remembering the day he almost convinced his Mum that he had been asked to represent his class. To be their spokesperson, should issues arise.

The job, had it been his, meant wearing a badge saying 'Council'. Sam was, as ever, hopeful. But the glory went to another child.

That evening he had told his Mum he had been chosen for the position. His Mum somehow knew, as Mums do, that he was trying to make her proud. Sitting together on his bed, she confided in him that she knew he was pretending.

They both cried...

Time stops for no one. It has a duty to fulfil, and the clock now said 5 a.m.!!

The slide to the Rainbow Skelter burst into life. A spectrum of colours lit up the darkness and the floor started to wobble.

Clamping the Certified Dyslexic Certificate between his jaws, Lexius took a great leap towards Sam, accidentally scratching him with his outstretched claws as he landed.

"Ouch!" bawled Sam, but Lexius didn't lose concentration. Seeing that the boy's top was tucked into his bottoms, Lexius frantically stuffed the very important Certificate into Sam's top, hoping it wouldn't fall out. He then sank his teeth into Sam's

pyjamas to drag the boy towards his only way home.

"Lexius, no!" yelled Sam.

"You have to leave, Sam. It's 5 a.m.!"

"No! Not without you, I won't go!"

"Your Mum, Sam, It has to be now!"

"Please come with me, Lexius, please...!"

"I can't, Sam. I can't leave Geri. I will never forget you, lad, you will always be my Sam. Now GO!"

Lexius lunged forwards and shoved Sam's chest, sending the boy toppling backwards, head-first down the Rainbow Skelter.

26

Sam's Mum woke with fright. The racket coming from the bedroom next door told her that her son needed comforting. She rushed to Sam's room.

"Sam sweetheart, Sammy darling, wake up! You're having a bad dream!"

Unravelling her boy from his bedding, she held him close.

"What on earth were you dreaming about, sweetheart?"

"I wasn't dreaming, Mum, I was in Letter Land with Geri and her Goblins! It was brilliant, Mum, they knew all about me and my problems at school. Geri says I'm Dyslexic, do you know what that is, Mum? It's

when people have trouble reading
and…"

"Yes, sweetheart, I know what
Dyslexic means."

"I flew through the sky with an
awesome dog called Lexius, you
would love him, Mum, he's brilliant.
Grandad H and Grandad Biscuit were
there too, in the Memory Pool."

"Gosh, you have had a busy night. I
don't think I dreamt of anything!"

Looking for the time on his bedside
clock, Sam's Mum caught sight of an
empty chocolate bar wrapper.
Deciding the damage had already
been done, her mouth closed. She
decided not to lecture him again
about sugar at bedtime.

Reaching out her hand to gently
sweep the damp hair from her son's
clammy forehead, she noticed some
pieces of paper crumpled up in a fold
of the duvet.

"Why have you got your report

from the Educational Psychologist in your bed, Sam? That report cost me a lot of money. I have a meeting with your Head Teacher on Monday morning and I don't want to hand it to her all scrunched up."

Sam grabbed up the document. "Geri had this printed for me when she told me all about Dyslexia."

"Ohh Sam... that's enough." His Mum was sounding a little weary now. "That's the report from the Educational Psychologist, he emailed it to me last night after he'd finished compiling the results from the test you sat with him last week at the Dyslexia charity. Believe me, lovely, I am so pleased that I finally trusted my instincts.

"Yes, you are Dyslexic, sweetheart, and the report shows that. It also shows what a smart little cookie you are too! Armed with this evidence we can hopefully move forward, getting you the help you need and deserve at school."

"But Mum..." Sam knew he had not

sat any test for Dyslexia – well not the conventional type anyway. This must be the work of Geri and the Goblins!

"Enough now, it's 5:20 a.m. and it's

Saturday. I need a little more sleep, sweetheart. Go back to bed for a while and when you wake up later I have a little surprise lined up for you."

"A surprise, Mum? What is it?"

"Later, Sam, back to sleep now."

Sam wondered if his Mum's parenting skills had slipped. Did she really think she could tell a nine year old boy he was having a treat and expect him to go back to sleep?

But Sam was so exhausted, he did go back to sleep!

He woke up to find his Mum downstairs in the kitchen making breakfast. Mmmm, pancakes with chocolate spread, his Saturday favourite.

He hugged her before taking his place at the kitchen table. Laying beside his juice was a flyer for the local dogs home.

"What's this?" asked Sam.

"It was in the letterbox last week, sweetheart. The dog shelter on Travis Road is having an open day today from 10 a.m. to 5 p.m., I thought we could go take a look around if you want, maybe we could bring a 'little someone' home, what do you think?"

"You mean get a dog, Mum? I can choose a dog?!"

"Yes, you can choose a dog. You deserve it."

Sam left his chair faster than the speed of light. Standing wrapped in his Mum's love, he knew this would be a great day.

27

Sam pestered his Mum for them to arrive early – in case everyone in town wanted to adopt a dog that day!

When they arrived, as he stood in the small but ample reception area of the dog shelter, Sam suddenly felt a little overwhelmed.

His eyes flashed over several posters decorating the walls. One of them warned of how dogs can die if left in hot cars, whilst others explained the importance of annual vaccinations and check-ups.

His Mum was talking with a lady from the re-homing team whilst filling out the relevant paperwork.

Sam could smell disinfectant and dog around them. He caught the warmth in his Mum's tone as she explained how they had owned a dog for many years, and now that enough time had passed, they felt ready to bring another into their lives.

Filtering through a set of double doors came the sound of canine activity as each unseen dog attempted to sing its way into their hearts and home. The shelter's choral society appeared to be in full swing today and filled the reception area. It would be tough leaving with just one companion.

Sam looked excitedly at his Mum, yet his heart felt heavy with attachment to Lexius.

"Any thought to what breed you may like, young man?" An older man wearing jeans and a long-sleeved shirt stood beside him, ready to offer guidance.

"One with a sense of adventure, please!"

"OK," said the man. "How about a Retriever or a Terrier? Now there's two breeds that will keep you entertained. Full to the brim with energy and curiosity they are!"

Sam had been so excited all that morning, but now he and his Mum were actually standing in the shelter he felt dispirited. All he could think about was a scruffy little black and white terrier called Lexius.

Sam fumbled for his Mum's hand, more for reassurance than confidence. She held it tightly, taking comfort that her son could still admit he needed her.

"Right then. Off we go, we just need to go through those double doors" said Tom – their guide's name was written on his badge, which was in the shape of a paw-print.

The shelter's residents were all

adorable in their own way. Several sat proud, not making a sound. Others needed to let everyone know they were there.

Two Labradors, older, lay resting, heads balanced perfectly on their front paws, calmly accepting of Sam's presence. Sam hoped they would find love in their twilight years.

Sam nudged his Mum and couldn't help smiling as a Border Terrier cocked his leg up the wall of his run, seemingly unaware he had guests!

Walking along, they greeted each of the inmates in turn.

There were big dogs and little dogs. Some were white with black spots, others had no markings at all. Some had short legs and long ears. Some had long legs and a pointy nose. Some had broad chests, housing barks deep and commanding.

Others were timid, staying further

back in their runs, as if they didn't wish to be thrust into the limelight.

Nearing the end of their tour, Sam wondered why the end run was empty.

"Did that dog find its forever home?" he asked.

"Let's hope so, shall we?" jollied Tom, waving his crossed fingers at Sam. "Left us yesterday afternoon, son, and sadly we already have another to fill his place."

Tom rubbed his chin, giving the centre's latest inmate some thought.

"He's out back, getting checked over by our resident vet. All newbies receive a wash and tidy-up before joining the gang. Have to make sure he's healthy, not carrying an ailment or infection of some sort. Poor little mite, abandoned last night he was. Left outside the centre doors."

"Can I see him please?" asked Sam.

"Sweetheart, there are so many dogs here already you can choose from, why not take another look?" said his Mum.

"I know, Mum, but I'd just like to see them all before we decide."

"He's a scruffy-looking little hound, but rather cute," said Tom,  just as the double doors squeaked open, prompting all three to turn round.

A member of the dog shelter team entered carrying a basket, a water bowl and a soft toy which she placed in the empty run.

Moments later the doors squeaked

again. Another member of the team entered, wearing loose fitting green scrubs. She was accompanied by a well groomed yet scruffy black and white dog. Her hand was cupped loosely around the loop handle of a blue lead attached to a very bright blue collar.

"Huh-huh-huh-**choooo!**"

Sam grinned as the lady wearing a generous smile stopped to wipe dog snot off her green trousers.

28

From the moment Lexius handed Geri his resignation, he lost the ability to speak with humans. His bone-shaped name tag was removed in readiness for his new life.

Geri knew how much a 'human' forever home meant to Lexius. She was also aware of how attached Lexius had become to their new friend Sam. After much discussion, reminiscing and many cuddles, Geri set the Dog Shelter's postcode into the Rainbow Skelter, hugged Lexius one more time, and lovingly pushed him towards his new life.

Lexius found much approval in his replacement, which to be honest hadn't been difficult. His successor, Dysia, was a chip off the old 'chilly nose' block, for she too had the advantage of detecting temperature change with her cute little wet nose.

Dysia just happened to be Lexius's great-niece and she had been paw-picked and personally trained by Lexius himself.

29

Warmth and splendour had returned to Letter Land. The Goblins, although it was their duty and great pleasure to help those in need, took a well deserved break from the production of frosty Flakes and chilly Letters. Enjoying the more amiable season, they made the most of their free time.

Conducting itself in a more relaxed manner, even the great red and gold train enjoyed the respite. Continuing its journey in a less robust approach, it once again transported Goblin folk up and down the mountainside.

The strained bellows of steam that had once roared from its almighty engine now entered the skyline in gentle, cloud-like puffs.

Summer flora had also returned to the hillsides and birdsong drifted sweetly from the hedgerows.

Geraldine, Squiggles and the Goblins enjoyed their well earned rest, but knew it was just a matter of time before the great chill of our world would return to theirs.

They knew from years of experience, that other children would regrettably already be on their Dyslexia journey, left unrecognised and alone. But for now though, monitoring the temperature of Dysia's button-like nose and to hope for the best would be all they could do.

Geraldine, Squiggles and the Goblins would always be ready to continue their quest. They would always be there for our children and their future.

30

The late October air snapped at Sam's bare knees, his breath visible from the onset of winter. Sam had spent time preparing Lexius for his new Monday to Friday routine by walking him the route to school several times each week.

He had taken time away from the loveable scruffy dog most days, hoping he would settle without him – and he had.

Lexius, as Sam named him, couldn't have looked more proud that first morning as he accompanied the boy to school, walking instinctively to heel, head and tail held high.

School had really listened to his

Mum this time, setting out different strategies to help ease the toil of his day. Expectations became more realistic, his timetable more manageable.

Sam's classmates had been made aware of his struggles and he was grateful for their new found empathy and tolerance.

Sam saw a new road opening up in front of him. It was long, of course, but the slope had already seemed to have plateaued.

"Is it three o'clock already, boy? I'm sure you have a built-in timer!" Smiling from the kitchen table, Sam's Mum shut down her laptop and put on her chunky sweater. "You always know when it's time to get your Sam, don't you. Come on then let's go!"

Lexius had given Sam's Mum a gentle nudge on her leg, before trotting out to the utility room. The clever little Terrier now gave a gentle tug on the end of his lead, whilst looking back at her.

Ten minutes later, running through the school gates, Sam and Matty were greeted by a very happy Lexius, and Lexius by two very happy boys.

Sam and his best human friend gave the little dog a big scratch behind both ears, before bumping fists and arranging to meet the next morning. Matty, still throwing jokey

comments at Sam, ran to where his Dad was waiting.

Sam took Lexius by his lead, gave his Mum a quick kiss and ventured on ahead, running and jumping without a care in the world.

*

Saturday morning had begun slowly. Lexius stretched out on Sam's bed, before rolling and falling off with a loud thud, causing Sam to laugh at the comedy of it all.

Instead of waiting for his pal to spring back up, Sam slid head first to where he had happily landed on the floor. Rolling on to his side, Sam's eye caught something unfamiliar. Now on his stomach, he wriggled his head and shoulders under his bed.

Out of reach in one of the corners, lay a blue light, and it was moving.

Sam wanted a closer look. Digging

in with both elbows under the bed, he wriggled himself closer to the light.

A sparkling blue Vapour had wrapped itself around the wooden leg of his bed. Opening out wide and bright, the vapour was allowing the boy a more detailed look.

Suddenly, Sam felt a tremendous urge to scratch at the scar on his left forearm. The unfortunate collision of claw and skin from where Lexius had desperately tried to get him home on time had left its mark.

Glistening before his eyes in multi shades of blue and silver, the merry Vapour hovered. Unlike his battle with the Memory Pool back on Letter Mountain, Sam had no recollection of what he was witnessing here. This was not a memory from his past.

Full of education and of winning, full of colour, of light and of happiness, this Vapour was his future.

Sam looked back over his shoulder

to catch the sight of his crazy scruffy black and white dog running round in circles, chasing his scruffy little tail.

Returning his attention to the Vapour, he saw it was nowhere to be seen now. Frantically scanning the carpet under his bed, Sam was desperate to catch another glimpse of what could be if he continued to believe in himself.

One big swoosh to the left and another to the right, Sam swept away a lieutenant-colonel complete with his regiment along with several super heroes including the Hulk and Spider-Man and tons of random pieces of Lego, but to no avail. The blue Vapour was nowhere to be seen.

Sighing deeply, lowering his head to the floor, Sam pushed himself back out from under the bed.

Sitting quietly with his knees huddled into his chest he watched

Lexius sniffing at something in the carpet.

The pooch's lips pulled back, his head shook left and right, and...

"Huh-huh-huh-**choooo!**" snorted the loveable hound.

It wasn't long before a smile so warm and wide spread across Sam's face to lift his spirit, brightening his eyes like diamonds.

The End

Help and Advice

Helen Arkell Dyslexia Charity
  Tel 01252 792400
  enquiries@helenarkell.org.uk

British Dyslexia Association
  Tel 0333 405 4555
  bdadyslexia.org.uk

Dyslexia Scotland
  Helpline 0344 800 8484
  info@dyslexiascotland.org.uk

Made By Dyslexia
  info@madebydyslexia.org

More House School
  Tel 01252 792303
  schooloffice@morehouseschool.co.uk

N.H.S. Dyslexia
  nhsdyslexia-nhs.uk

Other Resources

SEN Books
  senbooks.co.uk

Dayglo Books Gloria Morgan
  Tel 07948505628
  info@dayglobooks.com

Barrington Stoke Books
  Tel 0131 225 4113
  barrington@barringtonstoke .co.uk

Reader Pens C-Pen Reader
  thedyslexiashop.co.uk

'Afterword'

Dog-Lexius: A Tail of Two Friends . . . what a wonderful, inventive and imaginative story! Heartfelt and uplifting, Dog-Lexius will be a big hit with all kids (and adults).

It is indeed a pleasure and a privilege to be invited to write an 'afterword' for this book. The story is fascinating and gripping and is exactly the type of reader that children with Dyslexia need to get them into the reading habit.

This cleverly written tale (tail) by Susan Stewart can inspire and entertain, and will totally absorb children with Dyslexia. They will almost certainly want to read more about Dog Lexius. I really enjoyed the story line – and I am sure many young readers will connect with Sam and dream about 'tree surfing' with Lexius!

Dyslexia is now more openly talked about than ever before, but young children can still be puzzled and embarrassed by their difficulty in reading.

Needless to say, we as parents and educators, need to change this quickly and at an early age. It is heartening that Dyslexia is openly discussed in Dog-Lexius and in a 'matter of fact' manner highlighting that help is at hand in different forms.

I particularly liked the line: "You're Dyslexic, Sam, and I want to help you. I want you to understand why you are struggling at school."

This is exactly what young children with Dyslexia want to hear! The conversation between Sam and Lexius is like a cry for help and must echo the thoughts of many young children with Dyslexia.

Susan Stewart has a super turn of

phrase making Dyslexia meaningful – phrases like "The Blanket of Warmth for comfort", "The Memory Pool" and the "Letter Goblin to give you confidence" to read will help young children with Dyslexia feel optimistic.

Sentences like "I can't cure Dyslexia Sam but I can help you understand what is going on, a few changes can make your school life easier", and his mother's reassuring words – "what a smart little cookie you are too" – are all very reassuring to the sometimes bewildered Sam.

This is more than a reader, it is a novel – almost in the Harry Potter vein – one that can capture the imagination of readers with the fast moving and innovative story line, super illustrations that capture the moment, and a happy ending. This tale will show children that dreams can come true.

I would like to congratulate Susan

Stewart on writing this epic tale and Nick Awde for amusing, yet realistic illustrations that help the reader follow the story line with more than a tinge of excitement.

I feel certain this book will inspire and support young children with Dyslexia and will be welcomed by teachers and parents and cherished by young children!

Dr Gavin Reid
Author & psychologist

And more words...

This book hits the spot in so many ways! For a start, it is a romping good adventure story about a boy and a dog and a journey into space. It is impossible to guess what will happen next in this unpredictable, back-to-front universe.

But as well as that, the book addresses the oh-so-important issue of Dyslexia and the problems this can present for children when their teachers do not recognise the signs and do not understand the difficulties they cause. Still today, children are being dismissed as lazy, inattentive, not trying hard enough.

All teachers should hear alarm bells ring when a pupil is struggling to read fluently so that instead of condemnation, reassurance, encouragement and practical help are offered before a child begins to lose confidence and self-esteem.

So well done Susan Stewart for bringing this to the top of the schools agenda, and well done her magical creation Dog-Lexius for educating us all about what should – and what can – be done to help Dyslexic readers.

Gloria Morgan
Managing director of Dayglo Books

I loved reading this book! Sam and Lexius' adventures in Letter Land give hope and encouragement to all other children who find themselves in a similar predicament to our hero, who has Dyslexia. The story shows that people with Dyslexia can – and do – achieve amazing things if they believe in themselves and receive a little help and support along the way. If anyone reading this book needs any help with their Dyslexia, please do get in touch.

Andy Cook
Chief executive of Helen Arkell Dyslexia Charity